SHADOWS FALL
OTHERS OF EDENTON 1.5

BY BRANDY L RIVERS

Copyright 2013 Brandy L Rivers
Kindle Edition

All rights reserved. Without limiting the rights under copyright reserved above, no part of this publication may be reproduced, stored in or introduced into a retrieval system, or transmitted, in any form, or by any means (electronic, mechanical, photocopying, recording, or otherwise) without the prior written permission of both the copyright owner and the above publisher of this book.

This is a work of fiction. Names, characters, places, brands, media, and incidents are either the product of the author's imagination or are used fictitiously. The author acknowledges the trademarked status and trademark owners of various products referenced in this work of fiction, which have been used without permission. The publication/use of these trademarks is not authorized, associated with, or sponsored by the trademark owners.

Also by Brandy L Rivers

New Beginnings
Prequel to Others of Edenton

In Too Deep
Book 1: Others of Edenton

Coming Soon

Shadows of the Past
Book 2: Others of Edenton
I hope to have this out before the end of the year.

To keep up with upcoming releases
and news visit me at

www.brandylrivers.com
http://www.facebook.com/brandylrivers
www.twitter.com/brandylrivers

Table of Contents

Chapter 1	8
Chapter 2	22
Chapter 3	28
Chapter 4	35
Chapter 5	44
Chapter 6	47
About the Author	49
Reference Guide	50

Dedication

*To my mother who is amazingly supportive and a
wonderful mom.
I'm lucky to have you in my life, and to have your
help with my books
Love you, always and forever.
I hope my kids look up to me half as much as I look
up to you
You're the best.*

Acknowledgments and Thank Yous

Let me start by thanking my family. My kids are the best cheerleaders ever. It's pretty awesome when they tell me, "Mommy, you're the best writer ever." Granted, they aren't old enough to read my books, but it's still pretty sweet.

Magen McMinimy, you are a dear. If it wasn't for you I wouldn't have written this Novelette. Thank you for cheering me on, and helping me in the early stages. You're a rockstar.

LJ Baker, you never cease to make me smile. I love all your feedback on the early version. Now finish up working on your books so I can read the rest.

Amanda Keeney, you are a sweetheart, and amazing. Keep up the awesome work with your stories, and you're are a great beta-reader. I really do appreciate it.

Kristin Mayer, my Slater stalker, I love you, hon. You always make me laugh.

Claire C. Riley, I may have ignored one suggestion, but the next book, and In Too Deep should make that decision make sense. Your feedback was awesome. Thank you again.

All the ladies in Rivers Others, I love you, you really do build me up. I appreciate all of your posts in the group and all the support you all give me. Every one of you is amazing.

Chapter 1

Amethyst turned her key, but she didn't hear the click. The door was already unlocked. A shiver traveled down her spine as she stepped inside. She quietly set her purse on the table and closed her eyes.

He's here again. Her stomach plummeted and her heart thumped in her chest. *What will it take to make him stay away?*

She could feel Carl's presence, but she didn't know where he was lurking.

Her skin crawled as she made her way through her apartment. Turning around and leaving would be wiser, but she hoped she could grab a couple things and sneak out before he realized she was there.

A feeling of unease settled over her as she cautiously walked into her too dark bedroom. Her curtains were shut, but she had left them open that morning. Before she could turn around to leave, he was there, blocking her path.

Carl leaned forward, his pale hair falling into his deep blue eyes. "What's wrong, Amethyst? Aren't you happy to see me?" A wicked sneer twisted his lips.

Slowly, she backed away, wanting to put a little distance between them. It didn't work. He followed, backing her against the bed.

A startled gasp escaped her lips as she fell, and then quickly scrambled away, until her back hit the headboard. Carl crawled after her, and she flipped on the lights.

He wasn't very tall, but he had a good six inches on her and 60 pounds. His dark eyes drilled into hers. "Well, Amethyst. Don't you miss me, yet?"

"No." She was beyond sick of him, and all of his crappy power games. Pushing off the headboard, she shoved him hard.

With a surprised grunt, he landed on the floor.

A surge of adrenaline raced through her as she shot to her feet. Her hands landed on her hips as she glared down at him. "I told you we're through, Carl. How many times do I have to tell you to leave me alone? I'm done. That's not going to change."

The ugly smirk on his face faded into a mask of pain. She almost felt bad, but she knew he would smother her if she let him stay. He wanted to control her, to dictate every detail of her life. The only way to stop that from happening was to get rid of him.

There was a surefire way to make Carl stay away, but just thinking about it made her stomach sour. As a nymph, she could control people through sex. She could hold that part of her magic back now, but that wasn't always the case.

She still remembered Johnny, and her first orgasm from another person after her awakening. She thought she was in love with him at sixteen. They were in high school, and she hadn't even realized she *made* him *need* to spend every minute of the day with her.

It had been such a mess. First he wouldn't leave when it was time to go home, then his parents dragged him home. Less than an hour later, he had snuck out and climbed through her window. His parents dragged him away again, and he did it again.

She finally had to ask her Mom for help, which was embarrassing in its own right.

Using Carl's body to do what she wanted him to do just seemed wrong to her. It was an argument her mom had with her over and over again.

Mom would say, "Ame, hon, you've fucked him so many times, there's no difference. Just get it over with and he will be out of your life for good."

"That's just it, I don't want him anymore. I don't want to be with him just to make him go away."

"But he isn't going to leave you alone until you do. So suck it up, and at least give him a blow job."

She just needed to be more like Fallon and assert herself.

Carl climbed to his feet, peering deep into her eyes. She could feel his pain and almost broke down, telling him what he wanted to hear. Almost, but she reminded herself, *I'm stronger than that. I can do this.*

"Precious," he whispered. "I love you. Please don't send me away. I need you, always just you."

He didn't. What he felt was warped and twisted, but it wasn't love. She shook her head and pushed him toward the door. "No. You need to get a grip on reality, and leave. We're done. I can't do it anymore. You said you would give me whatever I wanted. Well, what I want is for you to leave."

"No." Desperation filled his eyes as he stepped closer. This time she didn't move. "Please, Ame, please."

"Go. Just please go before I yell for Mike." Thankfully, her neighbor was a werewolf. He would have no problem making a warlock leave. He was just next door and would come running in a heartbeat.

His chest heaved and his face turned red. "One day you'll realize you're mine," he promised vehemently, before storming out of her apartment.

Amethyst slumped on her bed as tears filled her eyes. She'd thought she loved him once, but somewhere along the way he started to go a little nuts. He seemed to be getting crazier by the day. She didn't know what to do about it either.

* * * *

Carl's heart ached as his rage built back up. Amethyst was his and would be until her dying breath. If she couldn't see reason, he would send her to the Silver Council. He knew she feared them, but maybe by the time they were through with her, she would trust *him* to take care of her.

Desperate without her, he forced tears to his eyes as he walked into the Silver Council headquarters in San Francisco. A young woman sat behind the front desk. Her golden eyes sparked as she glanced up at him. Her boredom dissolved into irritation.

She swept her onyx hair behind her ear, and sighed. "Do you realize where you are, *warlock*?" The last was said with distaste.

Doing his best to look pathetic, he sniffled and wiped the back of his hand across his tear streaked face. "Yes, but you're the only ones who can help me." A sob racked through him. "I've been fairy struck by a nymph."

The mage's brow wrinkled as she glared back. "A nymph you say? And why would she do this?"

"It's the only thing that makes sense. I can't go a moment without thinking about her, without wanting her. Now that she's through with me…," his voice broke, because his heart really was breaking. "Now that she's done with me, she wants me to suffer."

Her tone grew cold, and he felt the chill in the air. "You do realize that this accusation could mean her death, don't you? Are you sure you're fairy struck?"

He nodded gravely, praying that he wasn't sending Amethyst to her death. Still, it would be better to have her gone for good rather than see her in the arms of another man.

"We'll see about that. I'll bring you back to our lead investigator. Jarvis should be able to get to the bottom of this."

His blood ran cold at that name. There were some terrible rumors about what he liked to do to any nymph or siren in custody. Jarvis was rarely in San Francisco, and Carl never imagined he would be there for her captivity.

There was no going back though. He nodded slowly.

Her eyes narrowed as she stood up, towering over him. She walked him to the elevators, and motioned to another woman who hurried to the desk while she pressed the button.

"For the record, I hope you know what you're doing. If we find that you've lied about this, you'll be the one we punish," she warned.

"I know that." Carl did, but he also knew that if this didn't work, he would simply disappear.

The ride seemed to take forever, and he loathed

small enclosed spaces. If this hadn't been an urgent matter, he would have insisted on using the stairs. Before long, the little box opened and he stumbled into the hall with a shuddering breath.

The mage gave him a cold look before nodding to her right. She led him down the corridor to a metal door with a glass window. "Go on. Don't keep Jarvis waiting."

Carl stepped inside and took a seat in front of the stainless steel desk. The room was cold and uninviting with its bright white walls, and uncomfortable seating. There was no computer, no phone, nothing but the sturdy empty metal desk and two cold steel chairs.

He played the part of victim. With a whimper, he wrapped his arms around himself and began to rock back and forth, staring at the ground.

"Carl Umbra? I assume you have a reason to be here?" The mage sneered. Like most mages, they looked down on any other caster. Warlocks should never be dismissed, but mages were too self-absorbed to fear anyone.

"Amethyst Lakes knowingly seduced me, addicting me to her charms." He met the mage's dull black eyes as tears ran down his face. "I can't live without her." That part was true, but Amethyst did nothing to bind him to her. She was always so careful to avoid anything that would tie him to her.

Jarvis studied him like he was a specimen under a microscope, but Carl stared right back.

"Stupid warlock." Jarvis muttered before smirking. "We'll have to find her and see if what you say is true. I'll set something up to help you with your… addiction." He pushed himself back in his seat with a look of disgust. "I would think any caster would know better than to play with a fae slut without some form of protection."

* * * *

Finally, Amethyst had a solution that didn't involve naked play time to send Carl away. She took a deep breath and called Fallon. While the phone rang, she walked to the window to stare out.

Man, she hoped her closest friend, and practically sister was okay after the hell Brody had only hinted at.

Doubt started to creep in. Maybe she shouldn't be calling. Perhaps it was too soon. She almost hung up.

"Hi Amethyst." Fallon sounded so happy and it gave her a hope she hadn't felt in weeks.

"Fallon, are you okay?" She leaned against the wall and twisted the ends of her purple hair around her fingers.

"I'm fine. What about you? What's wrong?"

She smiled a little. Fallon really was like a big sister. Amethyst knew the timing was all wrong but she needed to set this in motion. She swallowed hard and blushed. "I hear you found yourself a good man." A sigh escaped her lips. "He sounds like a total sweetie." Just one brief call and she knew Brody truly loved Fallon. She could feel it over the phone, which was rare.

"Yeah. He is, and I'll tell you all about him later." Fallon was almost bubbly, which never happened. At least until her tone hardened. "But first, you're going to tell me what's wrong. I know that tone, sweetheart. What is it?"

The words rushed out of her in a stream. "Well, Carl won't leave me alone. He's stalking me. He shows up everywhere, begging me to come back. He hasn't done anything but say some really stupid stuff. I just… I don't know what to do."

Fallon cleared her throat. "So don't take this the wrong way. You have an option, and I know you know what I'm referring to. Just keep the option open and use it before you can't stand to be near him."

"I really don't want to go there." Her voice broke.

"I know, but you can make him want to avoid you without hurting him."

She pulled at her hair and looked blindly at the clouds. "Mom's been trying to get me to do that for months," she groaned. "The idea of using him like that just makes me sick."

"Sorry. If I knew Opal was on you about it, I wouldn't have gone there." She knew Fallon meant it.

"That's okay. I had another idea anyway," she said hopefully.

"Shoot."

"I was wondering if your new shop has an opening for a piercer. Between my mother and my ex, I think a move might be a good thing."

"We do. We don't have a piercer at all. Adam and Tomahawk turn green anytime someone walks in and asks for a piercing. The big babies." Fallon laughed. "So, just let me know when you think you're ready, and I'll set it up."

"Just like that?" She asked suspiciously

"Remember," Fallon told her. "Jess is up here, which means she probably already lined the job up for you. And if not, I'm in tight with the owner's brother, so don't worry about that."

Amethyst slid down the wall. She couldn't help wondering what Jess saw in her visions, and what she had already planned out.

Fallon broke the silence. "Are you doing okay? Really?"

"Yeah. Thanks for talking. I should let you go. Brody says you need your rest, though you sound good."

"I am good. But if you need to talk, you have my number."

"I do. Talk to you soon, Fallon."

"Bye Ame." Fallon hung up, and Amethyst tossed her phone on the bed, just in time for the pounding on her door to begin.

Before she could get to her feet, the door burst open, and three men stormed into her room with ugly sneers. She could feel their magic wash over her, so she sat there watching them.

"Amethyst Lakes?" One of them snarled.

At a loss for words, she nodded slowly.

"We're taking you in for questioning."

"For what?" She whispered.

"Jarvis plans to ask all of the questions. I'm sure he'll fill you in."

Terror froze her to her spot. Council mages always made her blood run cold, but that name was all her fears rolled into one. There was only one council mage she trusted, but she doubted bringing his name up would be any help.

* * * *

Carl watched from the dark alley across from Amethyst's building. Everything went as he expected. Three mages dragged a terrified Amethyst through the front doors and toward the dark van.

Her sparkling violet eyes went wide as she caught sight of him in the shadows. Her lip trembled as a tear slid down her face.

A pang of guilt twisted through his heart, but this was the only way to make her run back to him. If only she would realize she needed him every bit as much as he needed her. They shoved her into the back, and one of the mages climbed in with her before the other two hurried to the front and took off.

Waiting was the hardest part, especially with that sick fuck Jarvis in charge of the investigation. He would have her in his clutches, and he had a thing for breaking sirens and nymphs.

If Carl had known, he would have found another way. Then again, she would probably need his support after the terrifying ordeal. It may just work to his advantage

Chapter 2

The doors of the Van slammed shut, and a deep rough voice ordered, "Sit down now."

Amethyst didn't argue, just put her butt on the seat and wrapped her arms tight around herself.

The van roared to life, and she braced herself. She felt the brush of magic still the inside of the van.

"So quiet. Not going to try to use your lame little powers?" He sneered.

Everything clicked into place. Defeated, she dropped her head, letting her hair hide her face. Carl had gone to the council and lied. She couldn't stop trembling. Jarvis, just that name was enough to scare the daylights out of her, but Carl put her there.

Mom was right. I should have slept with him.

"I asked you a question," but his tone had softened. And then she heard the rustle of clothing, and then the seat dipped next to her. There was just a hint of concern. "You didn't. Did you? You could look me in the eyes right now and make me believe, but you won't. Will you?"

She shook her head, refusing to look. Under no circumstance would she give them anything to use against her.

"Hey, you're Opal's girl. Right?"

Amethyst turned away from the mage. Her mother would have used her power right then. Would have turned to him with her perfect acting skills as she gazed into his eyes, giving him what he wanted. Amethyst wanted nothing to do with half of her magic.

He leaned closer and she tried to shift away, but he didn't touch her. Another spell brushed past her senses and he breathed the words. "I'll call Preston. Maybe he can stop Jarvis."

Tears burned her eyes. He was probably lying, but without meeting his gaze she couldn't be sure. She knew that if she looked at him, she would use her magic to calm him. Then they could claim that she used her magic against them, breaking their laws.

There was another rustle of clothes and then the quiet beeping of a cell phone before she heard the faint ring. She couldn't quite make out the voice, but it could almost be Preston. The one mage she trusted. Mages weren't known for their compassion. It was probably a trick.

"You need to get to the San Francisco headquarters, and you need to do it now. We're bringing Opal's girl in, and it's Jarvis' case. You don't have long."

There was a beep and more rustling as the spell faded.

Another voice drifted from the front. "Don't play too much with the little nymph. Jarvis wants her to himself."

A new wave of terror drifted over her. *Please let this guy have a shred of decency, and please let him have called Preston.*

* * * *

The elevator doors closed. Amethyst closed her eyes and tried to breathe calmly. It wasn't helping.

Her hands trembled, and she was sweating even though she shivered against the cold.

The mage's magic enclosed them and his whisper was barely audible. "Preston is on his way. I'll try to stall until he gets here."

She finally found her voice, but it was quiet and shaky. "Why are you helping?"

"Nothing about you says you would purposefully do what you're accused of. You won't even look at me."

Her shoulders lifted in a shrug. "Carl is obsessed with me. He's been stalking me."

"And you wouldn't even use your magic to protect yourself against him?"

She shook her head. There wasn't a good answer for that.

He squeezed her shoulder. "I'm Jason. I'll do what I can to keep you safe. I just hope Preston gets here before Jarvis finds out you're here." He pulled his hand away.

She snuck a glance under her lashes. He had a baby face, warm brown eyes, and military short, brown hair. Jason seemed young and not fully grown into his frame.

"I'll do what I can," he whispered one more time. His concern only compounded her worries.

The doors opened and he gently took her arm to lead her down the hall and through big security doors. She could feel the buzz of magical energy from the wards placed there. The hallway had glass walls that looked into bland little white rooms with the bare essentials. Many of the cells were empty, but there was a variety of people and creatures.

It seemed as if they had been walking forever when he stopped to open a door. There was a toilet in the corner, a pedestal sink, a cot, and one small table between the bed and the slot in the wall that was probably only big enough for a tray of food.

He took his time opening the door, and gave her a slight nod before she stepped inside. She swallowed hard and took a seat on the corner of the bed. Her stomach dropped as silence closed in and doubt crept up on her.

Jason was still standing there when she looked up. His arms were crossed over his chest as he leaned against the door without a sound.

Time seemed to stand still and stretch out forever. It felt like an eon had passed.

"She's here?" A deep voice drawled as he stepped into sight. He looked older than any mage she could remember, which was supposed to be a sign of weakness. Most mages had enough power that they never seemed to age. This man had salt and pepper hair, and crowsfeet around his eyes. His voice was rough. "You didn't see fit to tell me you brought in the Lakes girl?"

"I was told to watch her," Jason answered automatically.

"By whom?" The tone was even colder, making her skin crawl. Amethyst curled into a ball in the far corner of her bed, instinctually putting as much room as she could between her and who she assumed was Jarvis.

"Magister Draecen."

"Now why don't I believe that statement?"

"It's the truth, Jarvis."

"You will move, or you will suffer my wrath."

Please, Jason, she begged silently. *Don't get yourself hurt over me.*

Amethyst peered through her hair at Jason. His chin lifted in defiance, and there was steel in his words. "You'll have to take that up with the Magister. I'm following *my* orders."

A wave of pain hit her as Jason was knocked away with a sweep of the other man's hand. The spell threw Jason down the hall and into a wall. Amethyst watched in horror as the young mage slid down the glass, clearly unconscious as he slumped onto the floor.

She squeezed her eyes shut as the door wooshed open. The sting of magic licked at her skin, but she held back her yelp.

"Get up." Jarvis' voice was harsh

She sat there, too stunned to moved. The shock of the whole situation had caught up with her. Her mother had recounted so many stories from Jarvis's victims, and now Amethyst was about to join that list.

"Get. Up. Now." Each word held a compulsion that slid right past her. Her own gifts were stronger, making her immune to his forced persuasion. If she wasn't so terrified she would have listened, but she couldn't make her body respond.

He made a tsking sound as all the air seemed to be sucked out of the room. Then he grabbed her arms roughly and dragged her off the bed and shoved her back against the wall. "Now look at me."

She shook her head as her heart tried to beat its way out of her chest.

Jarvis breathed against her ear. "You will do as I

say."

She tried to cringe away.

The temperature dropped a good twenty degrees in a split second. Jarvis was frozen to his spot, his fingers digging into Amethyst's arms too tightly. He wasn't even breathing.

"No, Jarvis. She won't do as you ask because you've been reassigned," Preston snarled.

Amethyst sighed in relief, but didn't dare move as Preston pried Jarvis' icy fingers from her. Then Preston dragged Jarvis out by his hair and left him in the hall.

She finally looked up to see the anger seething through Preston's icy blue eyes.

He spoke the words to another spell. The air charged and her breath caught as she felt the buffer surround the room. He spread his hands out, and bright lights traced symbols into each of the four walls and the door.

From the corner of her eye, she saw Jarvis rush for the door. An unseen force flung him into the opposite wall, making the glass shudder but she didn't hear a thing.

Amethyst clutched her hand over her mouth.

"Shh, quiet now. It's all right, Amethyst," Preston promised. His pale blue eyes searched her face carefully, and then the rest of her. He winced, and she glanced down to see angry red marks where Jarvis had held her too tightly. "That piece of shit," he snarled. "Are you all right? Did he touch you?"

Words still failed her but she shook her head no.

"He can't get in. No one can but me. I'll be here every day to check on you. You tell me if anything happens," he insisted.

"Okay," she whispered.

"I'll have to interrogate you later." His eyes closed and his jaw cracked he clenched it so hard. "I know you didn't do this, but I'll still have to question you."

"I know."

"Just sit down. Let me deal with Jarvis and Magister Draecen."

She sank onto the bed, and pulled her legs to her chest.

The room seemed to expand, and the pressure dissipated as Preston turned to step into the hallway. Another man had joined them. He had long dark hair tied back and a sinister goatee, but kind eyes as he glanced into the room.

"I take it Jarvis didn't believe that I put you in charge?"

"No, Draecen. I had to force him out of the room. No one will be able to enter that cell but me." Preston left no room for argument, but she knew that Draecen could order him to remove the spell.

Draecen glanced into the room and a frown tugged at the corners of his mouth. "See that she is unharmed. Jason assures me she doesn't seem the type to enthrall anyone. She wouldn't even use her gift to protect herself from three mages when they barged in on her."

"Sir, I was told this was my case," Jarvis snapped.

Draecen's cold gaze snapped to him. "And I'm telling you it is no longer your concern."

"I insist that you let me do my job."

"This is not part of your job. You are needed in the Appalachians at the present time. You'll find your current case on your desk. You're dismissed."

If Jarvis' face got any redder, his head might just explode. "As you command." He stormed down the hall and out of sight.

Draecen turned to her. "I trust Preston will get to the bottom of this. Unfortunately a complaint was made and we have to investigate." He turned away without waiting for a response and left.

Preston turned back with a hint of a smile and a wink before he followed Draecen. She still didn't know how long she would be stuck in the mages' prison.

* * * *

"What's your name?" The siren in the cell across from her asked. She smoothed a hand down her long straight pale hair. Her turquoise eyes held her gaze.

"Amethyst."

"I'm Lillian." A smirk twisted her lips. "And what are you in for?"

"My ex accused me of…." She sighed and looked away. She couldn't believe Carl could do that. "Of making him fairy struck."

"I take it he's bitter that you gave him up?" She snorted. "Men are such pigs."

Amethyst shrugged, but didn't bother arguing with the other woman. There were a few good men.

"I saw what Preston did for you. How did you manage that? Are you two lovers?"

She felt her blood rush to her face and knew she

blushed furiously. "No. Definitely not. I'm too young." Amethyst sighed, remembering her embarrassment when he told her that a decade before. "Besides, he was involved with my mother years before she had me. So that would be awkward." At least that was what he said, but she had been fifteen with a totally inappropriate crush.

"Ah. Opal Lakes. Yeah, she was always a wild one. At least until she settled down with that druid, Gabriel Sharpclaw. Is she still with him?"

A smile graced her lips. "She is. He raised me." Opal was still pregnant with Amethyst when they met and fell in love.

Another mage marched down the hall and Amethyst dropped her gaze. She heard the glass window slide open and then the scrape of metal on metal before heavy footfalls moving away.

"Dig in," the other woman told her.

Amethyst glanced at the food, and then over the siren as she took a bite of the fried chicken. Her stomach growled, but something told her not to touch the food.

"Eat up." The siren said. "The mages may not be the friendliest bunch, but their chef is excellent."

Amethyst gave her a weak smile. "Not hungry."

"Still need to eat" Lillian slurred as the drumstick slipped from her hand. Her eyelids dropped and in seconds she slumped to the floor in a heap.

Amethyst gasped and moved further away from the food. There was no way she was eating anything. Wards or no, she wasn't sure if Preston's spell could be broken.

Two mages calmly walked to her cell and

glanced at her, then her food before turning to the siren's room. Amethyst watched in mute horror as they dragged Lillian away.

Chapter 3

Two weeks in the same cell, and still no word when she would be leaving. Amethyst was losing hope. Preston had questioned her the day after she arrived, and Magister Draecen had been there. Both men believed her, but as Draecen explained, procedure called for them to keep her in the cell until they could prove she wasn't at fault.

She was curled up in the corner of her cot, hugging her legs tight to her chest. Her face was hidden by her knees. She just wanted out.

At least Preston made it bearable with his daily visits. Thankfully he brought her a little treat whenever he came by, and she did trust him. Jarvis hadn't been back down, but the siren had been taken four times in total. The first time was Amethyst's first night in the cell. The last three were in the last few days.

She was starving and so beyond tired. Those little snacks didn't go far, and she was afraid to sleep. Okay, she knew she was paranoid. No one had so much as stepped into the cell besides Preston, but she couldn't help worrying.

The door opened. She didn't bother to look up until the bed dipped. She peeked through the fall of her hair and saw Preston's pale blue eyes staring back at her. There was a lopsided grin on his face.

"Hey, Ame. Everyone still leaving you alone?"

She nodded, and even though she didn't dare hope, she asked, "Do I get to leave yet?"

"Sure do. I'm taking you home, but we need to talk."

Her head snapped up, but a frown pulled at the edges of her mouth. "Oh. About?"

Preston ran his hand through his hair before he took a look around. "Come on. We'll talk on the way."

He stood and held his hand out for her, which she gladly took. A wave of dizziness hit her when he pulled her to standing, and she swayed on her feet.

Preston's jaw clenched as he picked her up. She felt his magic buffer his voice from prying ears. "Did they feed you?"

"Yes, but....," she swallowed hard and looked up at him, "what if it was poisoned, or drugged?" Her eyes swept to the cell where Lillian was still asleep on her bed from that morning's breakfast. "I just… I couldn't."

Anger darkened his eyes. "I'll find out what I can." When he looked down, his expression softened. "You're okay though? Nothing happened that shouldn't have?"

She shook her head. "No one managed to get into my room. They left the food at the window and left."

"Why didn't you mention it?" he asked softly.

"Wasn't sure what you could do about it."

"Well, let's get you a real meal, and then we can talk."

* * * *

Carl sat in his shitty little Passat, watching the Silver Council's front doors. He sat there glaring as that bastard mage strolled inside with a purpose. Thirty minutes crept by as he waited, chewing his nails.

They would have to release her. It had been two weeks which was more than long enough for the Council to realize he had lied.

Then he saw her. She'd lost a little weight, her hair was limp and dull, and there were dark circles under her eyes. His hands cranked into fists, his uncut nails cutting past skin. Why the hell was she leaning into him? Why was his arm wrapped around her?

Amethyst is mine.

Preston took her to some fancy sports car that had to have some asinine price tag and opened the door for her. She disappeared behind the tinted windows, and Carl flipped around in his seat to follow.

Preston sped past his car, and before Carl could punch the gas, his windows were covered by black sludge.

"Fucking mage," he screamed as he turned the wipers on.

* * * *

Lunch had been awkward. Preston hardly said a word while they both ate an impressive amount of sushi. He was obviously brooding over something he was reluctant to tell her. They were in his car, *finally* heading back to her apartment.

"Nothing happened to you?" Preston asked again, more urgently than he had at Sushi Lane.

"No. Whatever protection you put up kept

everyone out. No one even tried to open the door." She sighed and looked back out the window.

"That siren, do you know what happened to her?"

Amethyst shook her head. "No, but it couldn't have been good." She glanced back at Preston. "So, now that you're taking me home, tell me what's on your mind."

His hands tightened around the steering wheel until his knuckles turned white. "Carl was waiting for you to be released from the council. He's been sitting outside the damned building every day or at your apartment, just waiting. He was going to follow until I created a diversion."

A shudder rocked through her, and she looked away. "Let me guess. You're going to suggest I bump uglies with him to get rid of him."

"That or let me get rid of him in a more permanent fashion. I don't trust that little shit. I never have. You do realize that filth is a warlock."

Amethyst snorted. "Barely. He has almost no magic to speak of. He's just desperate, and I don't even understand why." She rubbed her hands up and down her thighs and shook her head. "We fought constantly. Carl didn't even really talk to me. He just wanted me to agree to everything. I may not be as commanding as Fallon, but I don't let people walk all over me."

"Yes, but Ame, you are a beautiful young woman, and he's the type of bastard who wants to possess a beautiful woman." His gaze slid over to her for a second. "You deserve better than that."

She groaned. "I know. I'm not stupid. Why do you think I kicked his butt out?"

"Yet, he keeps coming back, and I know you don't want me to put him six feet under, so do us all a favor. Just fuck him and get it over with. He won't be back. I know you have it in you. It's just once, and trust me, there are worse things to suffer than a roll in the sack with someone you can't stand."

Amethyst's gaze swung back to him as her mouth fell open.

"No. Don't ask, kiddo. I'm not sharing those details. Just do it before he does something worse than sending you to the council."

A hysterical laugh bubbled up. "Don't. You stopped worse from happening with Jarvis. So don't." She dropped her head and closed her eyes. "I'll think about it. Okay?"

"That will have to do for now. I just don't want anything to happen to you." He reached over and squeezed her shoulder, sort of like her own brother always did. One more reason she had grown out of her crush.

"Thanks," she muttered.

"By the way, I warded your place against Carl. At least until you decide to let him in long enough to get rid of him for good."

She nodded as a feeling of defeat poured through her. The more she thought about it, the more she realized that was the best way to deal with him.

Preston parked the car. "I knew you wouldn't let me check the place for you. So, I made a trip and did it before I came to pick you up. I'll know if he tries anything."

With a glance his way, she smiled weakly. "I truly appreciate everything you've done. Thank you."

"Don't worry about it." He gave her hand a squeeze, "Just think about what I said. Okay?"

"I will, I promise." She climbed out of his Maserati and forced herself to keep moving.

Carl's eyes were on her, she could feel the caress of his gaze. It was the same sensation he gave her when he used to drag his fingers across her bare flesh. There was a time she had craved the way he watched her. Now it gave her the heebie jeebies.

The feeling faded as soon as the elevator doors closed. It was the first time in weeks that she could relax.

* * * *

Carl was hidden in shadow across the street from Amethyst's building, where he'd been waiting for nearly twenty minutes. He watched as that prick mage dropped her off at her door. He was ready to stomp over there and get payback for the sludge, but he didn't have the skills to go up against Preston. So he stayed out of sight.

Once the coast was clear, Carl sprinted across the street and up the steps to the front door. A jolt of electricity shot through him as his hand came in contact with the knob. He landed on his back and the air wooshed out of his lungs. His whole body trembled as he sat up, and then slowly stood.

What the hell was that?

He picked a wrapper up off the ground and tossed it at the handle. Nothing. He stood slowly, raising one finger and reached for the knob. The jolt promptly knocked on his ass again. This time he stayed down.

A dry chuckle snapped Carl's attention to the little old man who lived down the hall from Amethyst. He brushed past and said, "I heard the little lady tell you to leave her alone. Best be doing that, son." He slipped through the door and out of sight.

Carl launched himself to his feet and tried to slip through the open door, but was thrown onto the ground in a wave of blinding pain.

That fucking mage did this. It had to be him. Preston had been snooping around the building before going to the Silver Council.

He picked himself up, and made his way back to his car to think the situation through.

Chapter 4

A week later, Amethyst sat at the front desk of Painted On You, staring out the window, trying to form a plan to deal with Carl. She jumped when her phone rang and nearly dropped it in her haste to answer.

"Hello?" Her voice was shaky and Gabriel's eyebrow rose.

"Why haven't I heard from you in three weeks?" Fallon demanded. "Three weeks? You called about moving, and now you just don't call?"

"Oh fudge. I figured Gabriel told you." She felt it again, Carl's greedy eyes sweeping over her.

Gabriel gave her a pointed look, but his voice was quiet. "Couldn't tell Fallon anything when you still haven't told me where you were." Of course he hadn't asked, but he was the type to wait for someone to come to him with their problems.

"He didn't," Fallon answered. "Gabe just told me that Preston, of all people, assured him that you were okay. That was it. I found it awfully funny when Preston left Jamie to go back to San Francisco. Even stranger that he told Robert to translocate him when it makes him sick."

"Oh." She slumped back in her chair, and took a deep breath before letting it out. "Carl claimed he was fairy struck. He went to the council about it."

Gabriel stomped over to her, seething with fury. *Crap, probably should have broken that to him a little easier.*

"Want me to come up there?" Fallon just about shouted.

"No. I'm finally going to take care of it. I can't deal with him always being around."

"I'll take care of it," Gabriel growled the words.

She shook her head. "I don't want him dead. I just want him to leave me alone so I can move to Edenton." Her eyes closed and she winced as she directed her question to Fallon, "That is if you still think I could get a job?"

"Don't you worry about that, Ame. I have you covered there. If he does anything, call me so I can get there." Fallon's confidence was appreciated. Her sense of vengeance, not so much.

"Fine, but I'll be moving up just as soon as I take care of a few things. I already have my things packed." She did. The apartment didn't feel like home anymore, so she started packing right after Preston took her home.

"Hurry up and get here soon as you can. Since I know you won't do what you should." Fallon sighed heavily.

Amethyst's face scrunched up, and she balled her free hand into a fist. Everyone thought it should be so easy to sleep with her ex to get rid of him. The magic part would be, but she didn't think he could turn her on enough to make it work. She had an idea though, one that she really hoped would work.

She was finally tired of being underestimated, and heat infused her words. "Actually, I plan to screw him. It's the only way I can be sure he won't follow."

"Sorry." Regret laced Fallon's tone. "It's for the best though. Look, Ame, I've got to go. Call me later."

"I will," she promised, and hung up. Gabriel was still standing over her when she opened her eyes. He was the man who raised her. She couldn't read his emotions, probably because they were all warring with each other.

"The Silver Council had you for two weeks, and you didn't think to tell me that little slimy bastard put you in their hands?"

She swallowed hard, and shrugged lamely. "What could you have done about it?"

"Killed that fucking punk," he exploded. "In fact, next time…."

Amethyst stood up and shook her head. "No. Just let me handle this the way I should have before Carl went to them. Please. Maybe Mom will be proud of that."

The rage still burned in his eyes, but his expression softened as he pulled her into a hug. "She loves you, babygirl. I promise she loves you, and she respects your decisions, even if she thinks it would be better to just do it."

"It's an old argument, Dad. I just hoped I wouldn't have to resort to it."

"Can you do it?" He asked softly.

She put on a brave face. "Yes. I need to do this."

He nudged her chin up to look into her eyes. "If you can't, you call me. Or any one of us who love you, and we will take care of it."

She almost laughed. "Don't worry. I need to do this myself. I can do this." At least it sounded a heck of a lot more confident than she felt. "In fact, I know he's out there watching. So why don't you let me go, so I can lure him away, and get this over with."

Before Gabriel could say another word, she slipped out the front doors and walked calmly to her jeep.

* * * *

Carl watched as Amethyst left the shop and then made her way to her Wrangler. A bead of sweat dripped down his nose as he attempted to scratch his head through the itchy wig. Then he scrubbed a hand over the scraggly beard that had filled in since Amethyst was first taken by the mages.

He knew he looked ridiculous, but it helped him to stay out of sight. Her damned guardian mage always seemed to be nearby.

His girl would go home, and probably sulk some more. He just knew she was planning to slip away. He had overheard a couple of her neighbors talking about her packing her things a couple of nights before. That was when Carl placed a tracking spell on her jeep.

Take Her From You by Dev started to play. Amethyst was finally calling. He sat up straighter as he answered.

"Amethyst, is it really you?" His voice came out shaky. Had she changed her mind? Did she finally want him back?

"Can we talk?" she asked. Her voice was low and sultry like it always used to be before their problems started. "Please. I just need to see you."

"Of course. Where?"

"My place. Half an hour."

Anger flashed through him. "Will that spell still

be on the building?"

"No. I had to convince Preston this was best, but he finally gave in." She sighed. "I wanted to talk to you sooner, but…."

"It's okay. As long as you've come to your senses, we can work this out. We're meant to be together. You're meant to be *mine*, always and forever."

"We'll talk. Okay?" It sounded hopeful, but she didn't sound sure.

"I'll be there." He *would* convince her, one way or another. Shedding his disguise, he rushed to his car and slammed the door. Half an hour was enough time to shower and shave. He'd been such a mess since she shut him out that he hadn't taken care of himself.

* * * *

Amethyst was a ball of nerves, with a whole lot of anxiety and a little fear swirled in. She wrung her hands as she took another look through the apartment. All the boxes were in the closets. It looked a little bare, but it would have to do.

The phone rang. She almost smiled when she saw Preston's name on the display. "He's on his way up. Just scream if you need me, I'll be nearby," he promised.

That mental image made her shudder. "Seriously, Preston, that's kind of hinky. I know you mean well, but I'd rather not know you're close enough to hear me."

"Why's that?" Now he merely sounded amused.

She knew she was blushing. "I tend to be loud.

You may mistake my pleasure for something being wrong." Her face wrinkled up, imagining what he was thinking.

"Good to know." He chuckled. "I'll try to keep that in mind."

"I swear, you're such a perv," she muttered. "Look, he's going to be here any second. I need to go."

"I'll be close."

"Right, cuz that shouldn't make me feel weird about this at all." She hung up and hid the phone in her dresser. It would only cause a fight if Carl knew she had been talking to Preston. He was always so jealous about anyone who gave her the slightest bit of attention.

There was a sharp knock on the door and she jumped.

Breathe, just breathe, she told herself. She smoothed her skirt out as she walked to the door and let a few of her old Preston fantasies play through her head. He might be off limits, but she still thought he was awfully yummy. If she could just think about him, and not Carl, she might just be able to pull this off.

* * * *

Carl was just about ready to knock again when the door swung open. Amethyst still looked a little thinner than before her captivity, and there were dark circles under her beautiful eyes. A seductive smirk twisted to her pouty lips. "Come in. I need you."

That was all he needed to hear. That she wanted

him in her life. The anger slipped away as everything shifted back into place. He stepped inside and kicked the door shut before taking a step toward her.

She took a quick step back. "I've missed this." Walking backwards, she moved to her room as she pulled her shirt over her head and tossed it aside. Her full breasts spilled out uncovered, and he couldn't help licking his lips as he followed her.

Next, she unzipped her skirt, and let it fall to the floor. Her long purple hair fell around her, dancing along her hips as she sashayed back.

"I've missed you," he murmured as he rushed out of his clothes. "I've thought only of you."

"I know," she whispered as her fingertips trailed up her stomach, over the curve of her breasts to her taught buds with their little barbells.

His mouth watered as he watched her play. She laid back on the edge of the mattress. One hand slid back down and between her thighs while she spread her legs. Her head kicked back as a lusty moan escaped her lips.

He knelt before her. She was so sexy. Her delicate fingers dancing over her tiny clit. Her back arched when she pressed two fingers into her sleek heat. The whimper that rumbled out of her made his cock throb.

He missed her taste, and leaned in to lick her fingers as they withdrew. She made a needy sound that made his balls tighten. She wanted *him,* and he would give her everything. His tongue replaced her fingers, and her hips bucked against him. She was already so close just like she always was.

Her taste was unreal, sweet and all her. He took

his time, exploring until she was a writhing sweaty mess. He curled his tongue around her clit and sucked as he filled her with his fingers. She came undone.

Before her body stilled, he stood and plunged into her in one hard stroke that made her cry out. She gripped him and it was almost too much, but he needed her, and she needed him.

"Hard, fast," she screamed as her legs locked around his waist.

He grabbed her hips, lifting her for the right angle, and drove in and out of her little body.

"Look at me, Carl," she moaned. Damn, but she was already there again.

He locked gazes with her as she spiraled into release, pulling him with her. A deep calm enveloped him a second before the urge to flee swept through him. He couldn't stand to look at her as he came, but he couldn't look away.

Not mine. Leave her alone. Never again. Go, and never come back. The words whipped through his head like a whirlwind.

He stumbled back and gathered up his clothes before rushing out of the room.

* * * *

The door slammed, and Amethyst rolled onto her side as tears broke free. She'd done it. She let her power wash through her and into him, sending him away for good. Now she felt filthy and cheap.

Her phone rang, but she ignored it. She made her way to the bathroom and locked herself in.

It didn't matter who it was because she needed to

be alone. She cranked the water as hot as it would go and stepped inside. The compulsion she gave Carl was the safest way to end things, but she still felt guilty about using him that way.

Tomorrow morning she would load her jeep and drive away so she wouldn't have to see his face ever again. She didn't think she could handle knowing he was even in the same town as her.

Chapter 5

Carl wanted to stake a claim on Amethyst, but no matter what he did, he couldn't turn around and go back to her. The compulsion to leave was too strong to resist, and he had run to the hall before bothering to get dressed.

As soon as his shoes were on, not even tied, he scurried down the stairwell and out of the building like the hounds of hell were on his heels.

He saw Preston step out of the alley with his arms crossed over his chest and a smug smile.

Fear flooded Carl, and he hit the gas, speeding down the road on his way home.

Go. Never come back. Just leave her alone.

Then he realized it was Amethyst's voice screaming in his head. She forced the suggestion on him, she did this. She planted the suggestion in his head to stay away from her for good.

There was only one option left. He saw it in his dreams. The shadows would change him, but he would turn this around even if it killed him.

* * * *

Amethyst sat in the rocking chair with her arms curled around herself. She heard a knock on the door, and her heart stopped. She couldn't breathe.

I screwed it all up. He went to the council. Oh no.

"Come on, Ame," her mother called from the hall. "Open up."

She would almost rather have the council there. Amethyst forced herself to her feet, and trudged to the entryway. Dreading the conversation, she unlocked the door and only opened enough to see her mother's long silken white hair, and the concern in her opalescent eyes.

Before her mother could say a word, she said, "I can't talk, not right now. I need to pack. I need to go. I just… I just can't. Okay?"

"Baby, it's going to get easier," her mother told her.

"I know." She nodded, but she didn't believe it. "Look, I appreciate you stopping by, but I don't feel like talking. I just want to curl up and forget."

"Preston said he heard you crying."

She laughed sadly. "Yeah, well I told him to go away too. Just please, go. I'll be okay."

"You don't have to move now, sweetie."

"I do. I really do. I'll talk to you later." She tried to push the door shut, but her mom pushed back.

"You did the right thing," she said, but when Amethyst glared back, she finally turned to go.

The right thing? That was the right thing?

She felt like a two bit whore. Everything in her apartment reminded her of Carl. That last terrified look he gave her broke something inside her soul. She hated what she did, absolutely hated it, but she couldn't change it.

No matter what he did, she never wanted to see that look in his eyes. It just felt wrong.

* * * *

Carl tore through his apartment, looking for the ingredients to the spell he would need to cast. He had the archaic fae scroll spread out on the floor in the center of the room. He found the last of the herbs and brought them to the counter.

In a large bowl, he mixed the goats blood, salt and potent herbs. Then he spilled the contents in a circle on the floor. It was now or never, and he couldn't wait. He knelt in the center and began to read from the parchment.

As he finished the incantation, he closed his eyes. He never saw the shadow flow from the corner to pick up the dagger lying beside him.

He felt the sharp blade plunge into his chest as it buried itself to the hilt. His heart burst as he collapsed on the floor, grabbing for the dagger, but his hand kept slipping.

Cold seeped into his veins as the life drained from his body.

Chapter 6

The phone rang, and Amethyst jerked awake as she rolled off the couch and onto the floor in a heap of blankets. Terror twisted through her entire being, but she didn't know why. Something felt off.

The phone rang again and she jumped at the sound. She blindly reached for her cell and answered with a shaky voice. "This is Amethyst."

"Are you okay?" Preston's voice managed to soothe her jumbled nerves.

"Yeah, I was just sleeping," and having nightmares about a shadowy being she couldn't quite remember.

"Sorry." He took a deep breath. "I have some horrible news for you."

As warm as she was in the blankets and footy pajamas, she felt a chill all the way to her toes. "What happened?"

He sucked in a breath and let it out slowly. "The best we can figure is that Carl committed suicide."

"What?" she whispered, her heart started thumping a thousand miles a second. "Why? How?"

"It's the damnedest thing. He stabbed himself through the heart with some weird ass blade. His prints are the only ones here. There's a note, he'd been planning this for a while. I guess he finally got the guts to do it last night."

"Crap," she whispered. "I did that to him."

"No, babydoll. You did no such thing."

"I did. If I hadn't…," she let the words trail off.

"This isn't your fault."

"Thanks for calling. I'm going to leave a little early for Edenton. I don't think I can stay here anymore."

"Need a hand?" he asked gently.

"No, but thanks. Really Preston." She hung up before he could respond, and picked herself up. She needed to get away from San Francisco so she could start over.

Curious about what's going to happen to Amethyst? The story will continue in Shadows of the Past, Others of Edenton: Book Two

About the Author

Brandy L Rivers is the author of the Others of Edenton Series. In Too Deep and New Beginnings are already out nearly everywhere ebooks are sold.

Shadows of the Past will be coming out by the end of November. It will cover Hayden and Amethyst's story.

As an avid reader, Brandy has always loved writing. She became serious about it as a stay-at-home-mother. She has a file full of manuscripts she plans to edit and put out there eventually.

She lives in Western Washington with her husband and three kids, where she is already working on the future stories in the series.

If you are interested in receiving emails about future book releases, please sign up for her email distribution list by visiting her site at: www.brandylrivers.com

You can also find her on Facebook at: www.facebook.com/brandylrivers

And at Twitter: www.twitter.com/brandylrivers

Also at Goodreads. www.goodreads.com/brandylrivers

Reference Guide

Compulsion - Sirens and nymphs can force a suggestion on someone during sexual release.

Druids - Humans who possess mostly nature magic. They aren't as common as mages. Most tend to stick to other druids. They cast mostly earth and air spells, though most can manipulate fire and water. Druids can shift into most animals with practice.

Fairy Struck - This happens when a human has become addicted to a faerie's affection. This is rare and usually done on purpose or when the faerie is careless

Mages - Humans who possess elemental magic. They can either sling spells like weapons or heal, though it is rare for a mage to be a healer.

Nymph - There are water nymphs and wood nymphs. The water nymphs originated in faerie near lakes, oceans and rivers. Wood nymphs originated in the oldest forests. Most of their magic is powered by love, lust and similar emotions, and enhanced through orgasm. Unlike most faerie, they have no glamour and are stuck with their unusual coloring.

Others- Any being that isn't quite human. Werewolves, vampires, shaman, druid, mages, witches, warlocks, fae are just some examples.

Magistrate - Somewhat like the Silver Council's Sheriff, though their territory is larger than just one city.

Silver Council - Organization of mages. They are the governing force of most Others. Not everyone recognizes them as the law, but they do try to police all Others. The Silver Council is mostly made up of formally trained mages. They occasionally will employ other casters.

Silver Council Enforcer – The mages who police Others.

Siren - Sometimes called mermaids. They do change forms in water. Fine scales cover their skin, and they develop gills behind their ears. Their coloring often changes with this form. They have similar forms of magic to nymphs.

Werewolves - Specific type of wereanimal. A werewolf is created when a werewolf in either its beast form or half-man form bites and sometimes scratches a human. They are incredibly strong, and faster than a normal human. Powerful werewolves can not only shift into their wolf form but a form bigger than human, covered in fur with enormous claws and bestial head. Their sense of smell and sight are very strong, especially in their beast forms.

Ward - A spell that protects, sometimes keeps people from entering.

Warlock - A human who is highly sensitive to magic, and can cast a limited amount of magic. Abilities vary from clairvoyance, empath, telekinesis, and various other psychic abilities. Most are adept at potions that combine natural ingredients with magic.